WHO'S AFRAID OF GODZILLA

by Di Kaiju
Illustrated by Bob Eggleton
A Random House PICTUREBACK® Shape Book
Random House 🏠 New York

Monster Island
was the home of all the
Earth's giant monsters, and
every day the monsters played on
the island's sunny beach.

Gigan and Megalon wrestled. Anguirus chased Varan's tail. Manda swam in the ocean, and Rodan flew in circles high above the sand.

But not all of the monsters played together. One monster sat alone…

From the top of the island's tallest volcano, Godzilla watched the other monsters play. He wanted to join in the fun, but he knew they didn't want to play with him.

Godzilla was the biggest, strongest, and toughest of all the monsters. Because he was so powerful, the others were afraid of him. They always ran away when he came near.

One day, the monsters were having so much fun that Godzilla couldn't stop himself. He just had to join them! He jumped to his feet and ran down the side of the volcano, roaring with excitement. His howls echoed across Monster Island, shaking the palm trees and frightening the birds that lived in them.

"Here comes Godzilla!" Anguirus cried.

"Run!" Varan bellowed as he spread his
arms and legs and took off into the sky. Manda
hissed a warning, then ducked beneath the waves.
Baragon dug a hole and jumped inside. Gigan
and Megalon stopped wrestling and ran into
the jungle to hide. By the time
Godzilla got to the beach,
the other monsters were gone.

"All I wanted to do was play with them!" Godzilla cried angrily. He stomped his foot and roared. "If I can't make friends on Monster Island, then I'll go somewhere else."

Godzilla jumped into the ocean and disappeared beneath the waves.

When the other monsters returned to the beach, they wondered where Godzilla was going. Some of them felt bad because he was leaving. But a few were happy, especially Gigan and Megalon. Now *they* were the toughest monsters on Monster Island.

For a long time, Godzilla swam through the ocean. Finally, in the distance, he saw a great ship.

"Will you be my friend?" Godzilla called to the ship, filling the air with his mighty roar.

On the deck of the ship, the passengers and crew heard Godzilla's roar. They cried out in panic and ran for the lifeboats.

"Godzilla is coming!" they shouted.

Godzilla saw that the people on the boat were afraid of him, too, just like the monsters on Monster Island.

With a sigh, Godzilla swam sadly away.

Godzilla swam and swam through the ocean waves. Finally, he came to a great city filled with tall skyscrapers and lots of people.

Maybe he would find a friend here.

But when Godzilla climbed onto the shore, sirens began to blare. Tanks and airplanes came to chase him away. He howled in surprise as cannons were fired at him. The weapons could not hurt the mighty Godzilla, but he knew he was not wanted. So he turned and headed back into the ocean.

Godzilla swam underwater for many days, searching for a place where he could find a friend.

He saw whales and sharks and octopuses and even a giant squid. But, like the monsters on Monster Island, the creatures of the ocean depths were afraid of him.

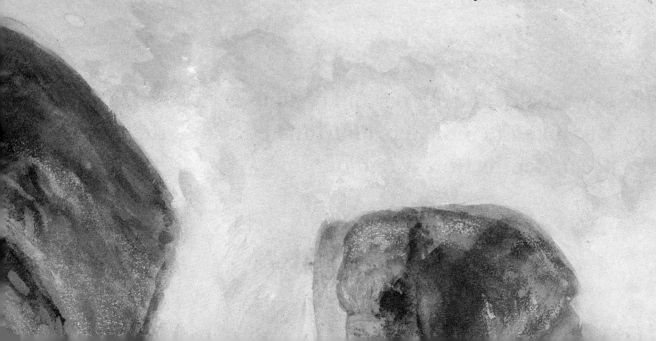

Finally, Godzilla arrived in a land with many different animals. Big ones and small ones—elephants, giraffes, and zebras.

"I'm sure to find a friend here!" Godzilla growled excitedly.

But when he came ashore, all the animals ran away in a dusty stampede. Once again, Godzilla was alone. He blinked. Was it the dust that made his eyes fill with tears?

As he turned to go, Godzilla realized he would never find a friend. With a heavy heart, he returned to Monster Island.

Meanwhile, back on Monster Island, Megalon and Gigan had taken over Godzilla's old ledge on top of the volcano. And the two big monsters began to bully the others.

Gigan frightened Varan into the sky. Megalon chased Manda to the far side of the island. Rodan flew away, and Baragon was so afraid that he burrowed underground and would not come out of his hole.

Anguirus was the only monster who didn't run away. "It's not right," he screeched angrily. "Things were better when Godzilla was here. At least Gigan and Megalon behaved!" Bravely, Anguirus climbed up the volcano to confront the bullies. But when he got to the top, Gigan and Megalon pushed poor Anguirus into the volcano's crater. The pit was so deep that he could not get out. Anguirus was trapped!

Suddenly, a mighty roar made Gigan and Megalon jump in surprise.

"Godzilla is back!" Gigan yelped in fear as the King of the Monsters charged up the hill. The two bullies ran down the other side of the volcano and hid in the jungle.

"Help!" Anguirus cried to Godzilla. "I'm trapped!"

All the other monsters heard Anguirus calling. With dread, they wondered what Godzilla was going to do to poor Anguirus.

To everyone's surprise, Godzilla stood quietly for a moment. Then he threw his long tail over the edge of the crater for Anguirus to grab.

"Hold on tight!" Godzilla cried. His muscles bulged as he dragged Anguirus out of the crater and set him down on the ledge.

Anguirus had never before been this close to the mighty King of the Monsters. He had always run away with the others when Godzilla came near. But Anguirus decided that Godzilla wasn't so scary after all.

"Are you all right?" Godzilla growled.

"Yes," Anguirus replied, "now that I have a big, strong friend like you to help me out of trouble!"

From then on, the other monsters played with Godzilla. Anguirus even asked Godzilla to wrestle. When Gigan and Megalon crept out of the jungle, they gasped, "Anguirus, aren't you afraid?" "Nah!" he replied. "Who's afraid of Godzilla?"